MW00818136

Raggsie Goes to Heaven

Ali Upton

Copyright © 2023 Ali Upton
All rights reserved
First Edition

NEWMAN SPRINGS PUBLISHING
320 Broad Street
Red Bank, NJ 07701

First originally published by Newman Springs Publishing 2023

ISBN 978-1-68498-556-2 (Hardcover)
ISBN 978-1-68498-557-9 (Digital)

Printed in the United States of America

To all those who have ever loved a pet.

Raggsie was a playful little white Bichon who had been together with her mom for many, many years. She remembered the day her mother had found her in the kennel. She had looked into the eyes of this woman and just knew that she had found the person who would give her a very special home. As the woman bent down to pet her, the little white dog jumped into her arms and gave her little puppy kisses. Raggsie thought, *This person will be my mother.*

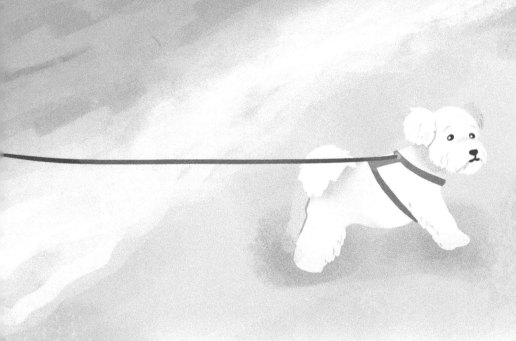

Over the years, Raggsie and her mom shared so many
adventures. Together, they visited pumpkin farms, climbed hills,
ran along the beach, played in the water, and so much more.

Sometimes, they took car adventures. Raggsie loved those car trips because she had her own special car seat that made it easy for her to look out the window and catch breezes. Wherever they went, there would always be snacks in the car—chocolate for Mom and cheese for her.

On one trip, they had stopped for ice cream. Raggsie had loved having her very own vanilla cone. She licked the ice cream slowly and enjoyed every bit of the cone. It was so yummy! But when they got home, she was not feeling well, and her little belly had the "gurgles." Her mom took her to the vet who said that Raggsie couldn't have ice cream anymore because her tummy couldn't handle it. On their way home from the vet, Mom had reminded Raggsie that she might not be able to have ice cream, but she could always have pizza!

5

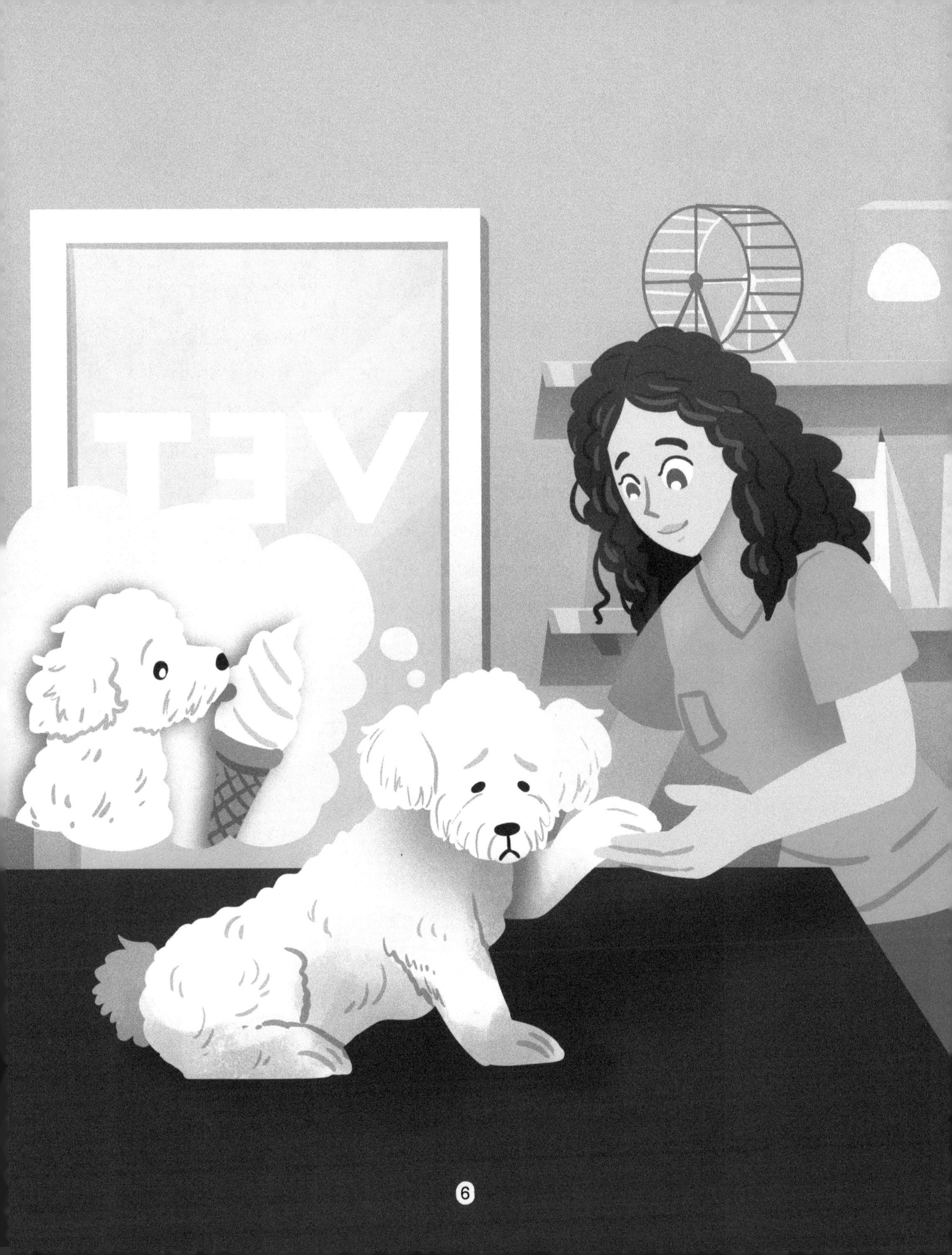

Those trips and treats continued for many, many years. As Raggsie got older, she began to notice that she couldn't run or jump the way she used to. Her long walks became shorter, and she no longer liked playing in the snow. Raggsie's eyes could not see clearly anymore, and she had trouble hearing sounds and voices.

Then one afternoon, a few days after Christmas, Raggsie let her mom know that it was time to go to the special place that her mom had told her about—a place where there was no pain, no sadness, and no tears. Her mom had called that place Heaven. Her mom never wanted Raggsie to be in pain, and Raggsie's aches were getting worse. As her mom held her closely in her arms, Raggsie could feel the teardrops falling from her mother's eyes as she whispered, "Go, my precious puppy. I will see you again. Look for the white staircase and climb."

Raggsie snuggled against her mom and shut her eyes. At that very moment, she found herself at the bottom of a staircase made of fluffy white clouds. She remembered her mother's words and began to climb. As she hopped from cloud to cloud, she noticed that her legs were not in pain and her body did not ache anymore. She looked around and was surprised that she could see clearly again. Raggsie felt very happy!

It was a long staircase, and every few steps, she would turn to look for her mother. She would stop and wait, stop and wait, but Mom wasn't there. She heard birds chirping, and she smiled. She looked for her mom to tell her that she could again hear the smallest of sounds. Just then, a little bluebird flew past her, and Raggsie continued up the fluffy white cloud staircase. Soon, she could see the top of the stairs. But the last step was very high! She was a wee little dog, and her legs were very short She jumped and jumped again, but she could not make it. *How will I get to the top when my little legs can't jump that high?* she wondered.

All of a sudden, she heard a voice say, "Come, little one, I will help you." Raggsie looked up and saw a beautiful figure standing above her. At first, she thought it was another bird because she could see wings. As she looked more carefully, she could see that it was a glowing figure dressed in a white flowing gown. Beautiful golden rays seemed to shine all around her. At that moment, a hand reached down and gently picked her up.

"Oh, thank you," Raggsie said. "I was struggling with that last step, and I didn't think I could make it."

"Yes, I know, but do not worry. That is the last struggle you will ever have."

"Where am I? And where is my mother? We were always together, and she would be upset if she knew I was alone," Raggsie asked the angel.

"Don't worry, puppy. Your mother knows where you are, and one day, she will be with you again."

Raggsie asked again, "Where am I? And who are you?"

"You are in Heaven, and I am here to help you. I am your very own angel."

Raggsie had heard her mom talk about angels, but the puppy didn't realize that they would be so beautiful. Raggsie looked around and saw that this new place was beautiful, too. There were lush green trees and grassy hills, sparkling ponds and streams, and flowers of every color. While Raggsie was looking around, the angel put down two bowls. One bowl had delicious cool water that the puppy quickly lapped up. The other was a big bowl of creamy vanilla ice cream.

"Oh, no," Raggsie said, "I cannot have ice cream. It makes my tummy gurgle."

"Don't worry, sweet puppy, you are in Heaven, and you can have anything you want. There will be no more gurgles here!"

Hearing that good news, Raggsie gobbled up the yummiest ice cream ever.

VANILLA

WATER

After Raggsie had finished eating, the beautiful angel said, "Come, let me show you around."

As they strolled through Heaven, they came to a grassy area with hundreds of purple wildflowers. Raggsie's eyes opened wide in surprise. There playing in the field were the special friends she had played with when she was growing up.

She saw April, Duffy, and Muffin, the golden retrievers. Running alongside them were Nicky the collie, Jack the Irish setter, Molly the chocolate lab, and Ginger the boxer. Even Lucky the black cat joined in their play. Raggsie had missed them when they had gone away. Mom had told her that they left to go to Heaven and that she would see them again one day. *Mom was right*, Raggsie thought.

"Before you go and play with your old friends, here comes a surprise," said the angel. Charging across the field came a smiling German shepherd. Raggsie knew immediately that it was Girl.

The German shepherd had been Mom's puppy, and Raggsie had seen so many pictures of her. Mom had told her that Girl had climbed the fluffy white staircase many years before Raggsie was born. With Girl at her side, Raggsie joined her old friends. They played and played and stopped for treats. Then they played some more.

Raggsie was so happy to be with her friends in Heaven, but she still had thoughts of her mom. She missed her and remembered that her mom had told her they would be together again. What Raggsie didn't know was that time in Heaven is different than time on earth. Many years had passed on earth even though it didn't seem that long in Heaven.

One day while she was playing with her friends, Raggsie had this strange feeling in her belly. *Oh, no*, she thought, *have the gurgles come back?*

But this feeling was not a bad feeling. It was a feeling that something happy was about to happen. She looked around and started to sniff the air, but everything seemed okay. Then she looked around and sniffed again, and there in the distance she saw a figure approaching. She wondered, *Could it be? Could it really be?*

There standing in the field of flowers was her mom who opened her arms, and Raggsie jumped into them. As she covered her mom's face with kisses, she looked lovingly into her eyes, and the little Bichon asked, "Did you climb up the fluffy white staircase?"

"That is the staircase that everyone climbs to come to Heaven," her mother told her.

"Will you have to go back down and leave me?" Raggsie asked.

"No, my little puppy. We will stay here together forever in this beautiful place called Heaven," her mom told her. "We will have many more adventures, and we can both eat all the ice cream we want!"

From that moment on, there was no pain, no sadness, and no tears. There was only happiness for the little white Bichon and her mom who would be together in Heaven forever.

About the Author

Ali Upton is a retired NYC special education teacher. She created and authored the monthly newsletter *Headstrong* for the NYS Brain Injury Association for over twenty years. She is currently practicing equine and canine massage therapy as a volunteer in Connecticut. She feels fortunate to have had many dogs that brought much joy to her life and the lives of those around her.

CPSIA information can be obtained
at www.ICGtesting.com
Printed in the USA
JSHW050524200223
37774JS00001B/4